JUMBO
Coloring and Activity Book

MATCHING

FOLLOW THE PATH

USING THE LETTERS, IN ORDER, FROM THE WORD **ASSEMBLE,**
FOLLOW THE CORRECT PATH TO FIND YOUR WAY THROUGH THE MAZE.

START

A	X	M	B	L	Y	Q	N
S	S	E	Q	E	A	S	Z
E	R	T	N	S	G	S	E
R	M	E	A	E	L	B	M
L	B	S	S	A	S	X	
E	S	E	M	K	N		
A	S	L	B	T	R		
N	N	E	A	N	I		

FINISH

© 2019 MARVEL

DOT TO DOT

CONNECT THE DOTS TO FINISH THE PICTURE.

HOW MANY WORDS?

HOW MANY WORDS CAN YOU MAKE USING THE LETTERS IN
HAWKEYE

EXAMPLE: Awe

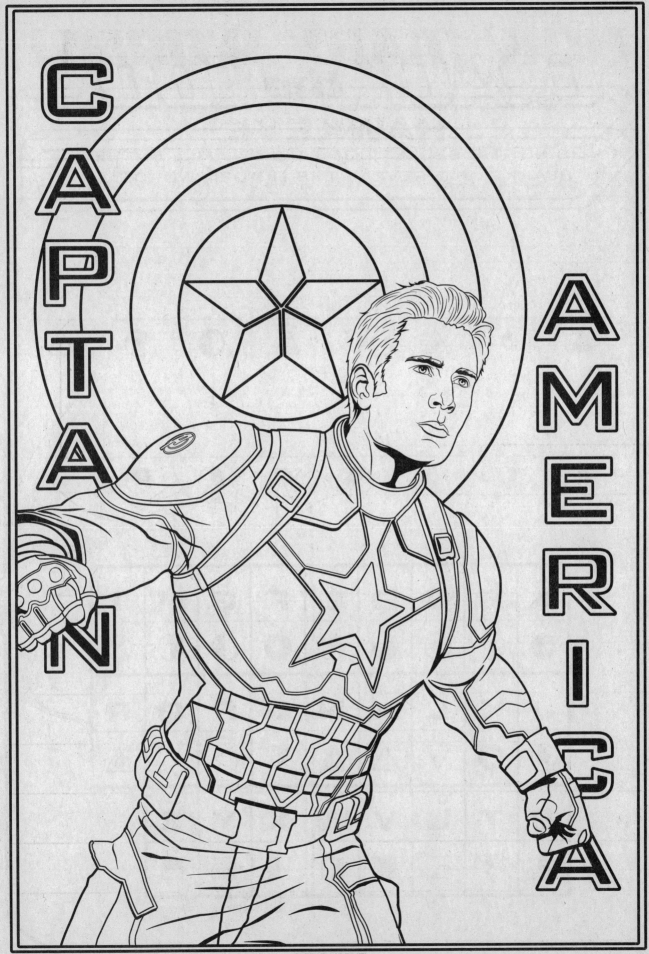

CRACK the CODE

USING THE SECRET CODE BELOW, FILL IN THE BLANKS AND REVEAL THE HIDDEN WORDS!

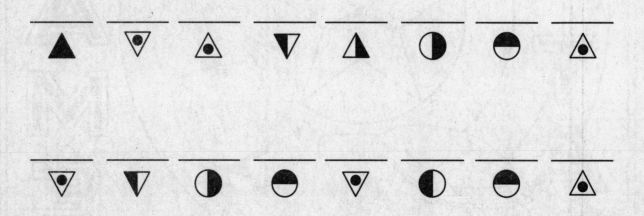

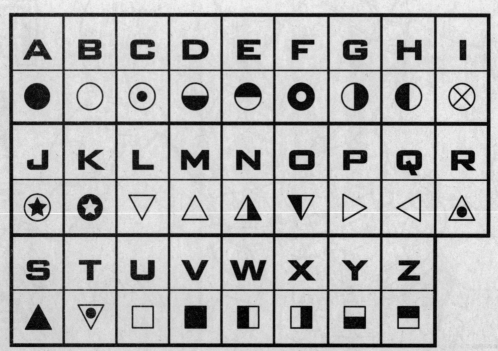

© 2019 MARVEL

IMPOSTERS

THREE OF THESE AVENGERS ARE IMPOSTERS. THE ONE THAT IS DIFFERENT IS THE REAL War Machine.

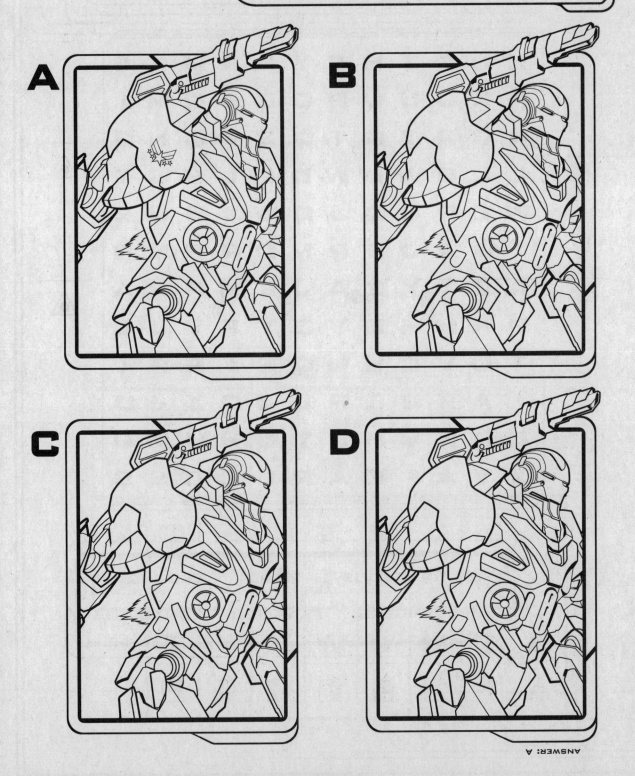

A

B

C

D

WORD SEARCH

SEARCH UP, DOWN, AND DIAGONALLY
TO FIND ALL THE WORDS.

```
X H C Z H F Y B R M K S
P K U U U P O E C Q M I
N C R T G T Q E F Q N G
L L O W J W D E L S J T
W E P U Q J O O V S U E
T G A J R R N D R F N N
P E T X E A J E M P P A
D N M H B V G Y F V J C
T D V C H N Q E I R P I
I A K U E P L J O X J O
C R K V M B T Q H U M U
X Y A F E A R L E S S S
```

COURAGEOUS   HERO   LEGENDARY

AVENGERS   FEARLESS   TENACIOUS

Draw

IRON MAN

USING THE GRID AS A
GUIDE, DRAW THE PICTURE IN
THE BOX BELOW.

CROSSWORD PUZZLE

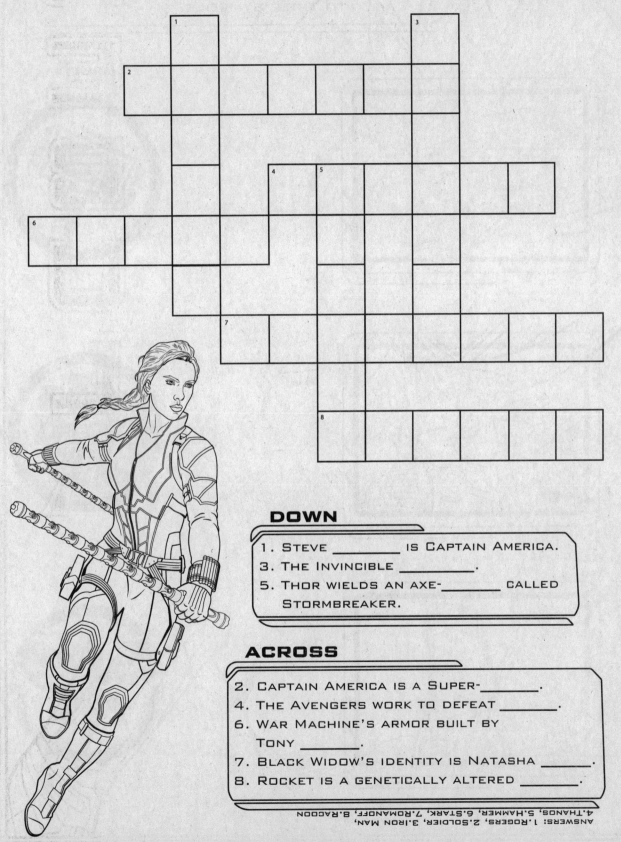

DOWN

1. STEVE _____ IS CAPTAIN AMERICA.
3. THE INVINCIBLE _____.
5. THOR WIELDS AN AXE-_____ CALLED STORMBREAKER.

ACROSS

2. CAPTAIN AMERICA IS A SUPER-_____.
4. THE AVENGERS WORK TO DEFEAT _____.
6. WAR MACHINE'S ARMOR BUILT BY TONY _____.
7. BLACK WIDOW'S IDENTITY IS NATASHA _____.
8. ROCKET IS A GENETICALLY ALTERED _____.

ANSWERS: 1.ROGERS, 2.SOLDIER, 3.IRON MAN, 4.THANOS, 5.HAMMER, 6.STARK, 7.ROMANOFF, 8.RACOON

MATCHING

TIC-TAC-TOE

Use these tic-tac-toe grids to challenge your family and friends!

Squares

EXAMPLE

Taking turns, connect a line from one symbol to another. Whoever makes the line that completes the box puts his or her initial in the box. The person with the most squares at the end of the game wins!

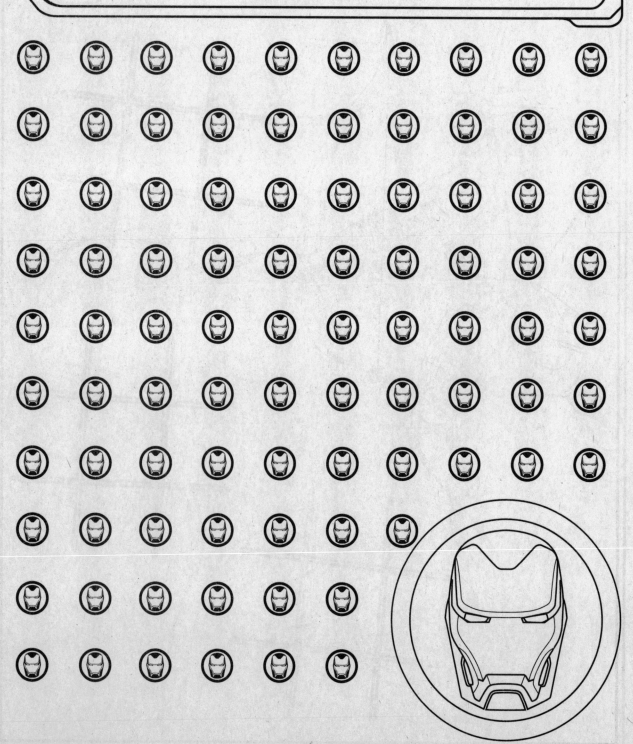

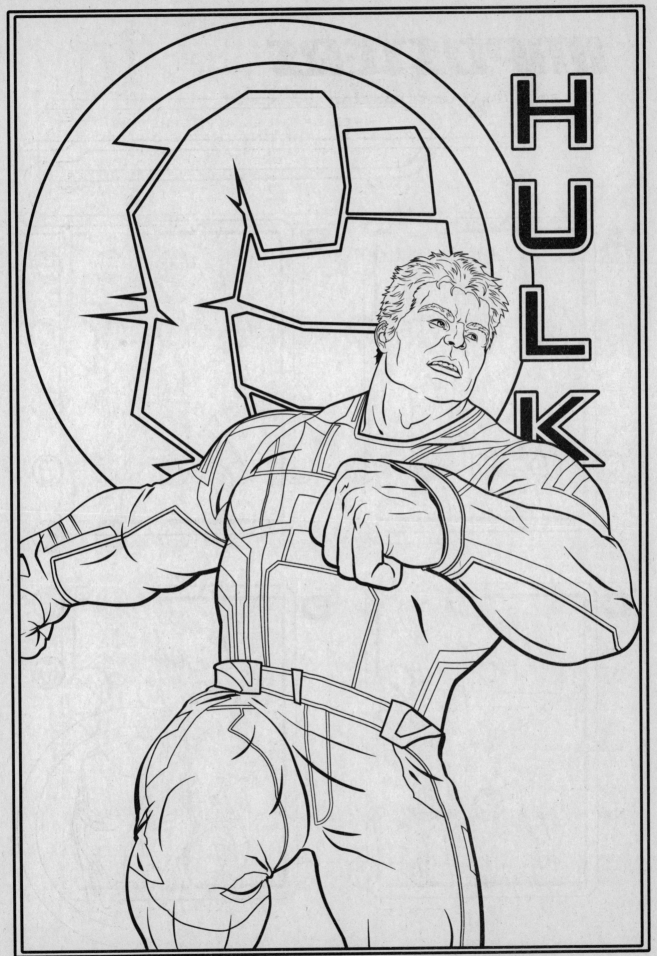

IMPOSTERS

THREE OF THESE AVENGERS ARE IMPOSTERS. THE ONE THAT IS DIFFERENT IS THE REAL Black Widow.

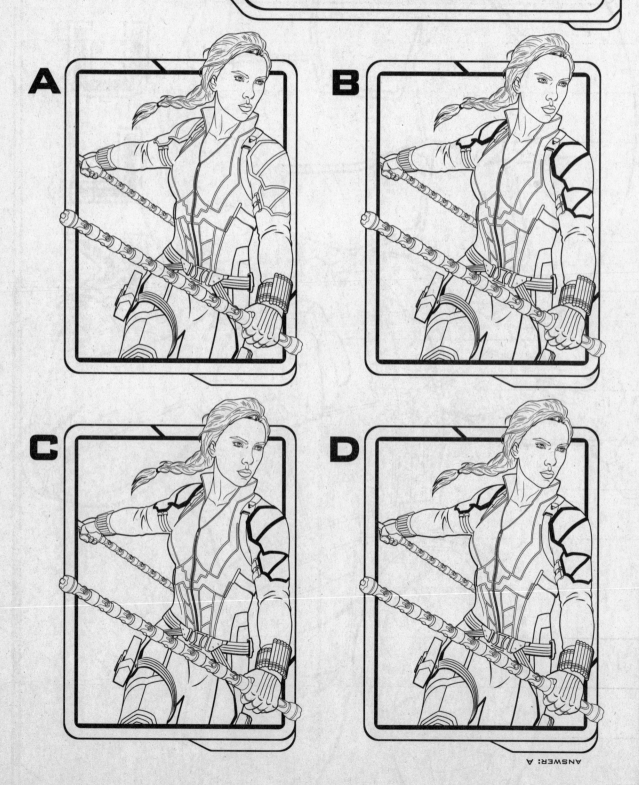

HOW MANY WORDS?

HOW MANY WORDS CAN YOU MAKE USING THE LETTERS IN

WAR MACHINE

EXAMPLE: CHIME

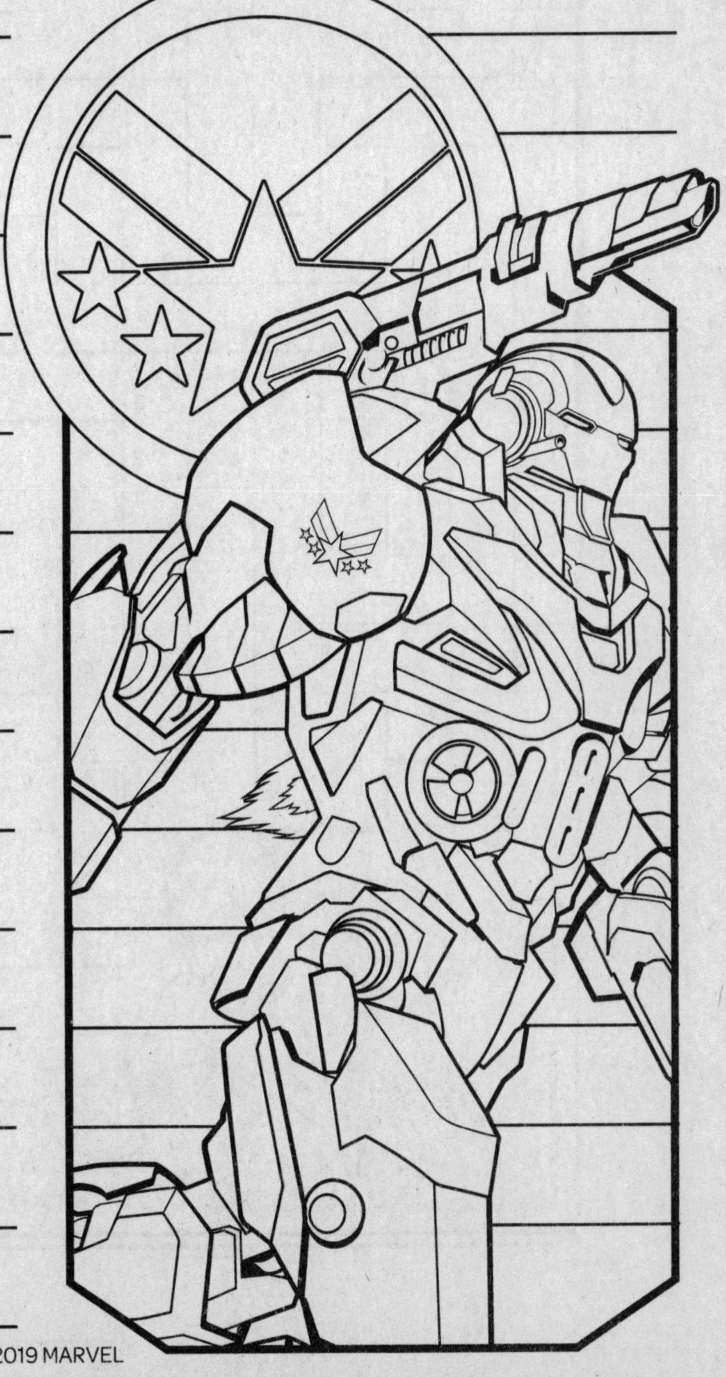

MAZE

HELP ANT-MAN FIND HIS WAY
THROUGH THE MAZE.

FINISH

START

WORD SCRAMBLE

USING THE WORDS FROM THE LIST,
UNSCRAMBLE THE LETTERS TO CORRECTLY
SPELL THE NAMES AND WORDS.

OMRNNIA

_____

KDIBWAOLCW

_____

RTCEKO

_____

MRAAICTNPCIAEA

_____

SLRAEESF

_____

GUOASREOUC

_____

WORD LIST...

CAPTAIN AMERICA	FEARLESS
ROCKET	BLACK WIDOW
COURAGEOUS	IRON MAN

CRACK the CODE

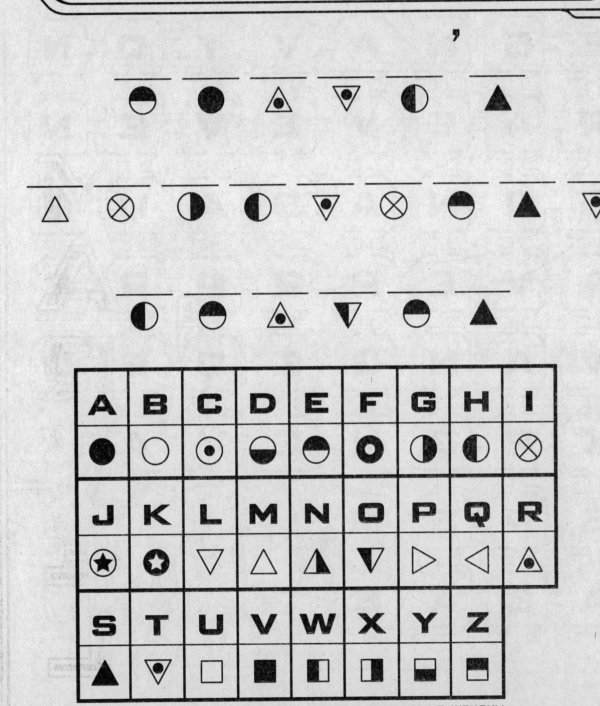

© 2019 MARVEL

FOLLOW THE PATH

USING THE LETTERS, IN ORDER, FROM THE WORD **AVENGERS**, FOLLOW THE CORRECT PATH TO FIND YOUR WAY THROUGH THE MAZE.

▼ START

E	G	N	A	V	Y	Q	N
R	A	E	V	E	V	E	N
S	R	N	A	S	A	U	G
A	V	E	P	R	R	P	R	E
V	A	N	G	E	Q	S	D
K	P	G	N	E	V	A	
S	R	E	M				
A	S	A	E				

↓ FINISH

MATCHING

DOT TO DOT

CONNECT THE DOTS TO FINISH THE PICTURE.

HOW MANY WORDS?

HOW MANY WORDS CAN YOU MAKE USING THE LETTERS IN
STORMBREAKER

EXAMPLE: Arm

_____   _____
_____   _____
_____   _____
_____   _____
_____   _____
_____   _____
_____   _____
_____   _____
_____   _____
_____   _____
_____   _____
_____   _____
_____   _____
_____   _____
_____   _____
_____   _____
_____   _____

CRACK the CODE

USING THE SECRET CODE BELOW, FILL IN THE BLANKS AND REVEAL THE HIDDEN WORDS!

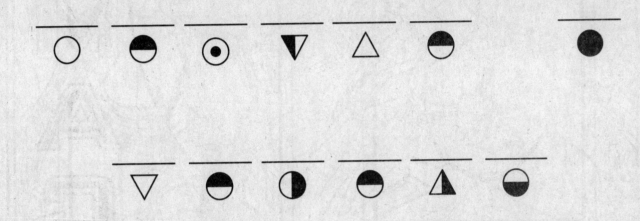

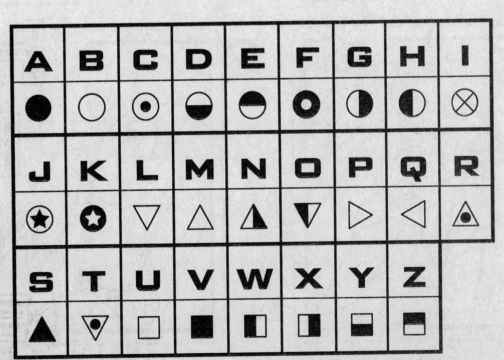

IMPOSTERS

THREE OF THESE AVENGERS ARE IMPOSTERS. THE ONE THAT IS DIFFERENT IS THE REAL Nebula.

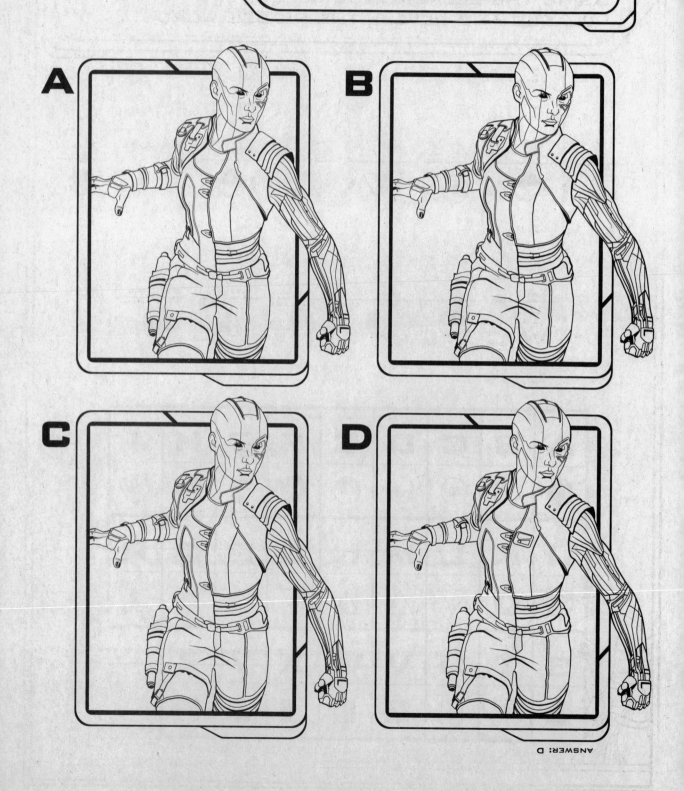

A

B

C

D

WORD SEARCH

Search up, down, and diagonally
to find all the names.

```
E Q D Z H U D O O L U G
T Q X X J V M A R V E L
X W G C V N Q U H Y R K
C A S U R A X X P U Z N
G R Q Y G T G Z Y G L R
H M I R O N M A N F E K
B A G R O C K E T W F Z
W C T G P Y R V I K T I
G H E F B M U O G A I L
R I F N D D Z W P P P D
Z N E Y A V Y N Q T D O
E E B L A C K W I D O W
```

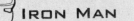

Iron Man	Hulk	Black Widow
Marvel	War Macine	Rocket

Draw
BLACK WIDOW

USING THE GRID AS A GUIDE, DRAW THE PICTURE IN THE BOX BELOW.

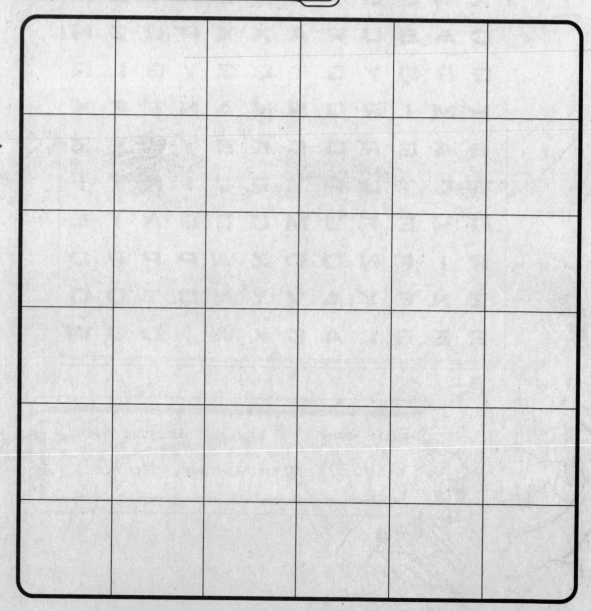

ROCKET

CROSSWORD PUZZLE

DOWN

1. _____ COMES TO HELP AFTER A CALL FROM NICK FURY.
4. FORMER THIEF TURNED HERO.
5. THOR IS THE GOD OF _____.

ACROSS

2. NEBULA IS THE _____ OF THANOS.
3. THE INFINITY STONES ARE IN THE _____.
6. THE AVENGERS ARE EARTH'S _____.
7. THANOS CONTROLLS THE _____ STONES.

MATCHING

DRAW LINES TO MATCH THE AVENGERS
TO THEIR SYMBOLS.

TIC-TAC-TOE

Use these tic-tac-toe grids to challenge your family and friends!

Squares

EXAMPLE

TAKING TURNS, CONNECT A LINE FROM ONE SYMBOL TO ANOTHER. WHOEVER MAKES THE LINE THAT COMPLETES THE BOX PUTS HIS OR HER INITIAL IN THE BOX. THE PERSON WITH THE MOST SQUARES AT THE END OF THE GAME WINS!

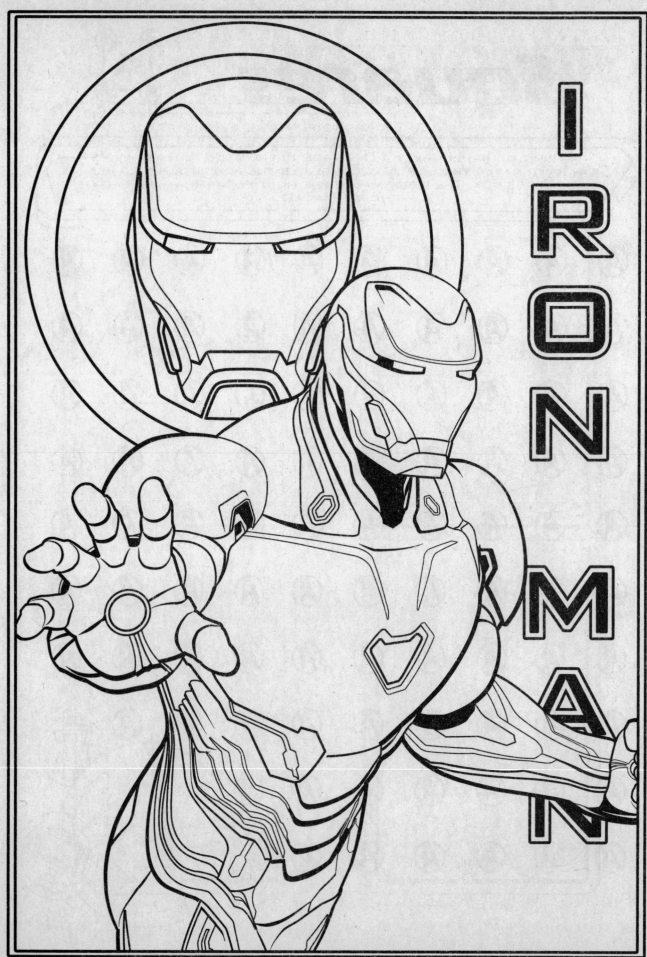

IRON MAN

IMPOSTERS

THREE OF THESE AVENGERS ARE IMPOSTERS. THE ONE THAT IS DIFFERENT IS THE REAL CAPTAIN AMERICA.

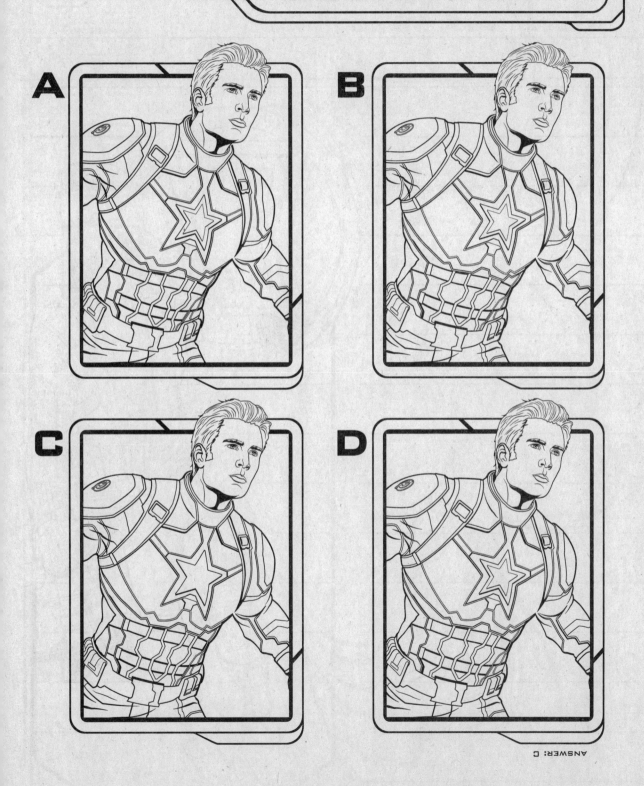

ANSWER: C

HOW MANY WORDS?

HOW MANY WORDS CAN YOU MAKE USING THE LETTERS IN
NATASHA ROMANOFF

EXAMPLE: Staff

WORD SCRAMBLE

NDAAGURI

_____

UKHL

_____

MIRCAAHWEN

_____

NAEDYRGLE

_____

EEWYHKA

_____

SREILDPHAE

_____

WORD LIST...

HAWKEYE	LEGENDARY
WAR MACHINE	HULK
GUARDIAN	LEADARSHIP

MAZE

HELP ROCKET FIND HIS WAY THROUGH
THE MAZE.

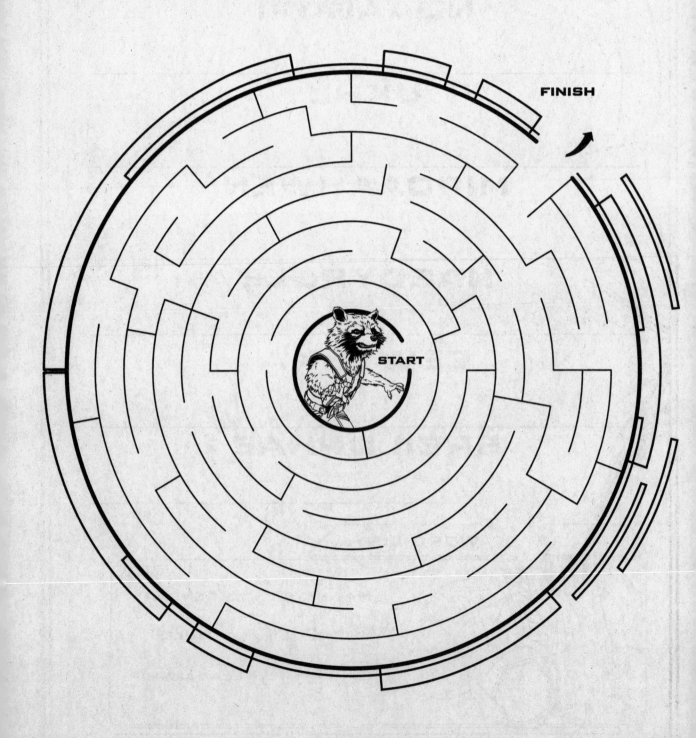

FINISH

START

THOR

MATCHING

© 2019 MARVEL

CRACK the CODE

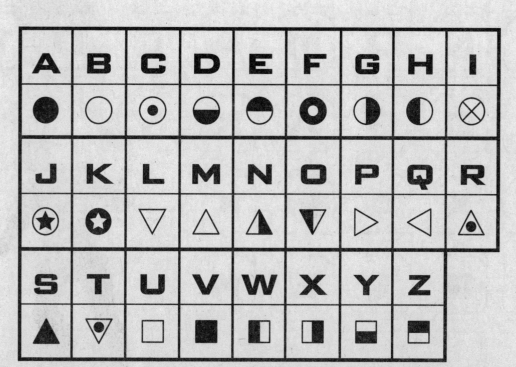

ANSWER: BE COURAGEOUS

FOLLOW THE PATH

USING THE LETTERS, IN ORDER, FROM THE WORD **ENDGAME**, FOLLOW THE CORRECT PATH TO FIND YOUR WAY THROUGH THE MAZE.

START ▼

```
Z  R  G  T  G  D  N  E
J  G  D  Q  A  G  H  E
M  A  N  N  M  E  E  A
E  D  E  E  E  P  N  R
E  N  D  M  A  G  D  D
K  D  G  A  K  V
G  X  A  M  K
N  R  I  E  N
```

▼ FINISH

© 2019 MARVEL

DOT TO DOT

CONNECT THE DOTS TO FINISH THE PICTURE.

HOW MANY WORDS?

HOW MANY WORDS CAN YOU MAKE USING THE LETTERS IN
BRUCE BANNER

EXAMPLE: Can

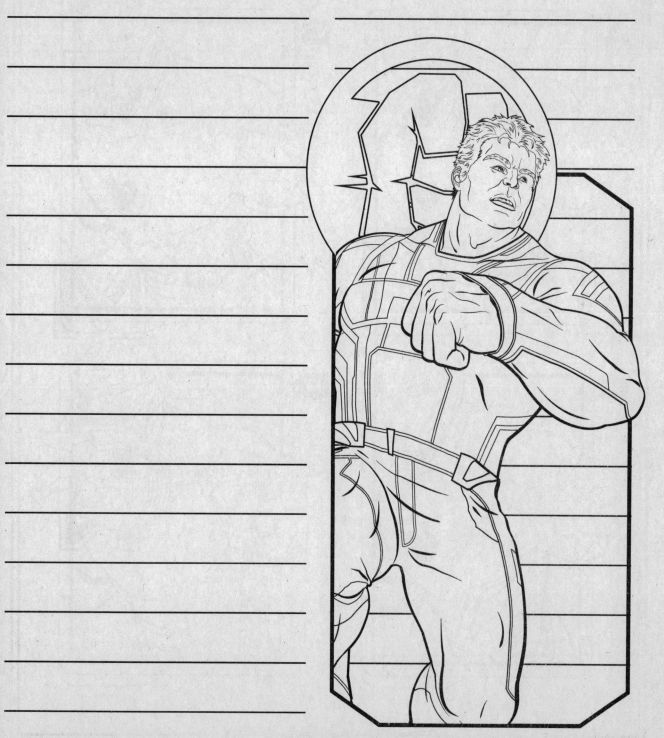

IMPOSTERS

THREE OF THESE AVENGERS ARE IMPOSTERS. THE ONE THAT IS DIFFERENT IS THE REAL IRON MAN.

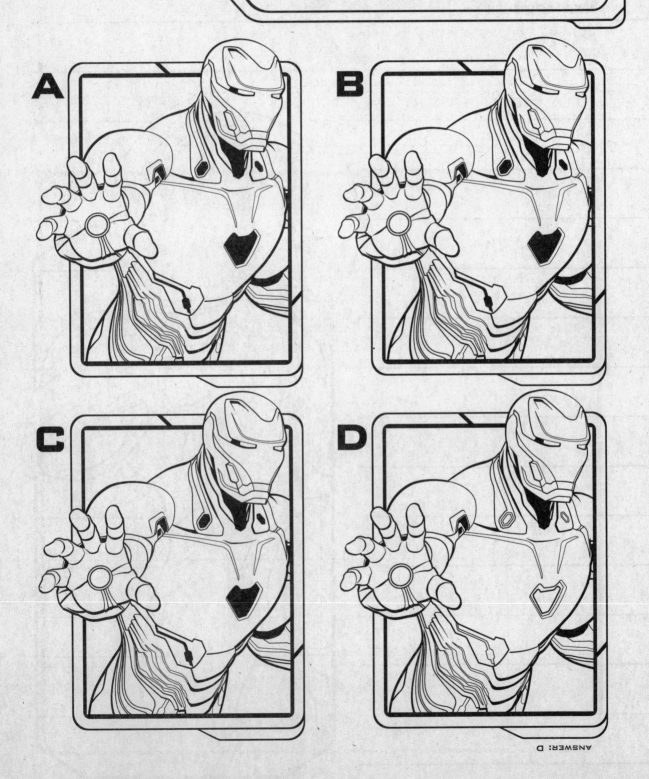

Draw

CAPTAIN AMERICA

USING THE GRID AS A
GUIDE, DRAW THE PICTURE IN
THE BOX BELOW.

CROSSWORD PUZZLE

DOWN

1. Green Hero.
3. Team of Heroes.
4. Captain Marvel's identity is Carol _____.
5. Skilled Archer of the Avengers.

ACROSS

2. Master Spy.
6. Bruce _____ is the Hulk.
7. The Super-Soldier, Captain _____.

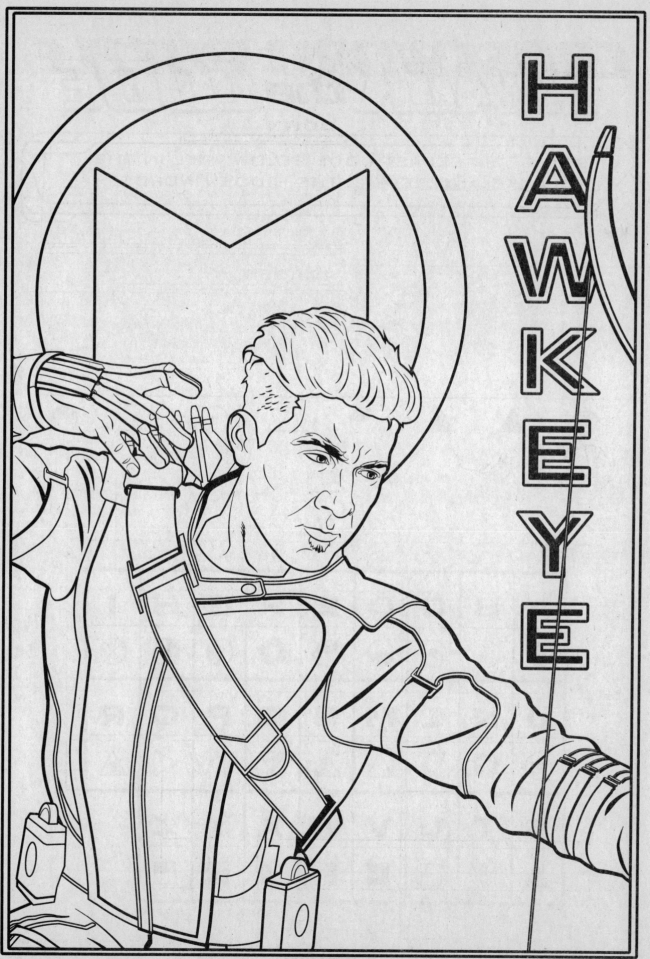

CRACK the CODE

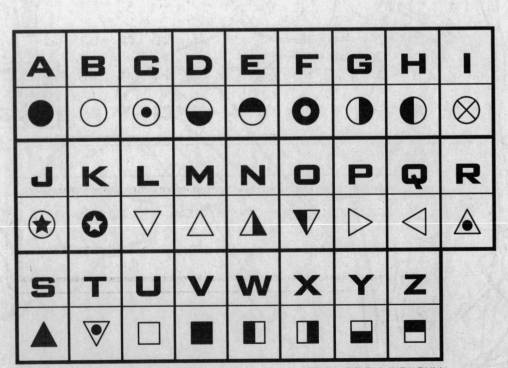

WORD SEARCH

Search up, down, and diagonally to find all the names.

```
S L K U G Z O E C J Q E
F G M R F Z Y N P J X K
Q O N D B E I J Q U D O
J A V B K A Z Z T A A W
F R W W T U Z E W P N Q
V H A P Q I A P A E T Y
E H A M C T M N M X M D
L C D G H H E L D T A C
Y A T X H O R D E P N T
Z P P S B R I X S E U J
Z Y I Q L E C M H A W Q
N E B U L A A Z O T M O
```

CAPTAIN	AMERICA	ANT-MAN
HAWKEYE	THOR	NEBULA

TIC-TAC-TOE

HOW MANY WORDS?

HOW MANY WORDS CAN YOU MAKE USING THE LETTERS IN
AVENGERS ASSEMBLE

EXAMPLE: Green

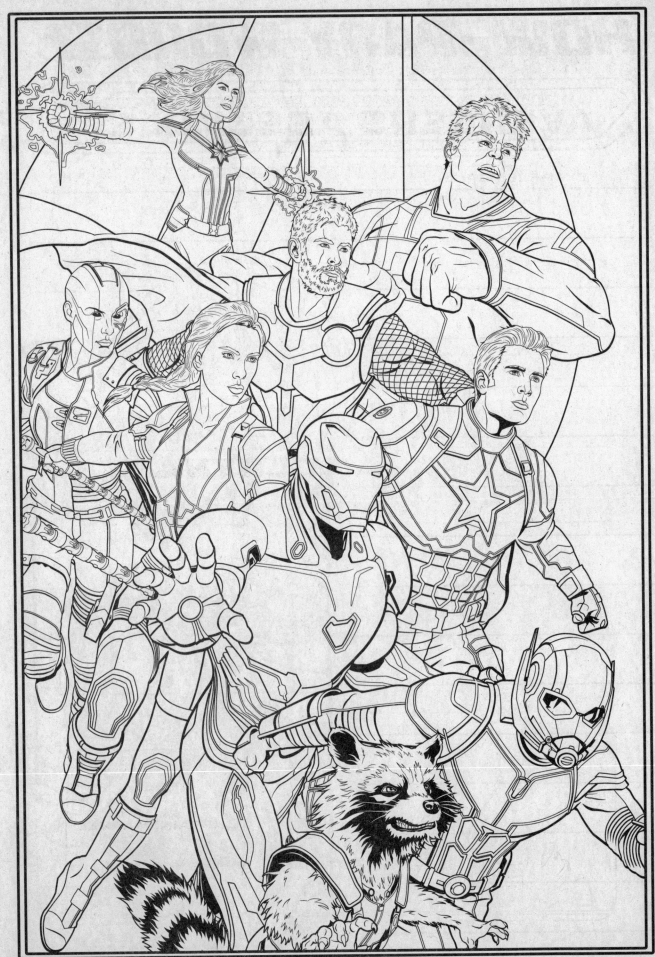

WORD SCRAMBLE

Using the words from the list, unscramble the letters to correctly spell the names and words.

REHFRTSOAHEOE

MNTNAA

CNIEOATSU

IVPAEAMCLRTNA

OHTR

UABNEL

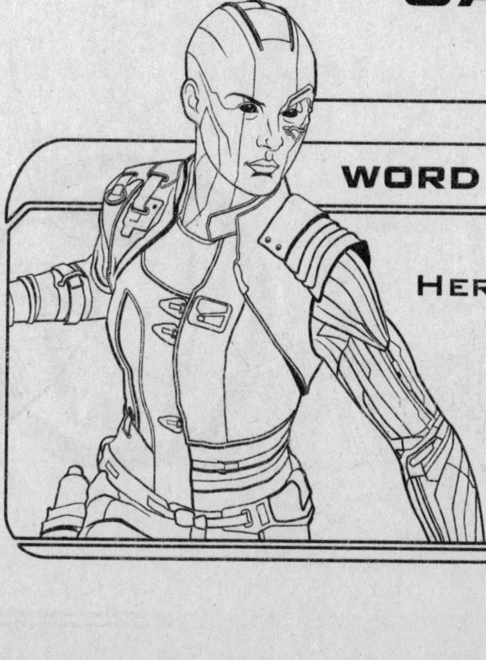

WORD LIST...

Heroes of Earth

Nebula

Thor

Captain Marvel

Ant-man

Tenacious

MATCHING

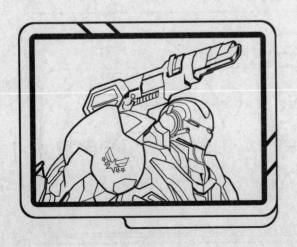

Squares

EXAMPLE

Taking turns, connect a line from one symbol to another. Whoever makes the line that completes the box puts his or her initial in the box. The person with the most squares at the end of the game wins!

IMPOSTERS

THREE OF THESE AVENGERS ARE IMPOSTERS. THE ONE THAT IS DIFFERENT IS THE REAL THOR.

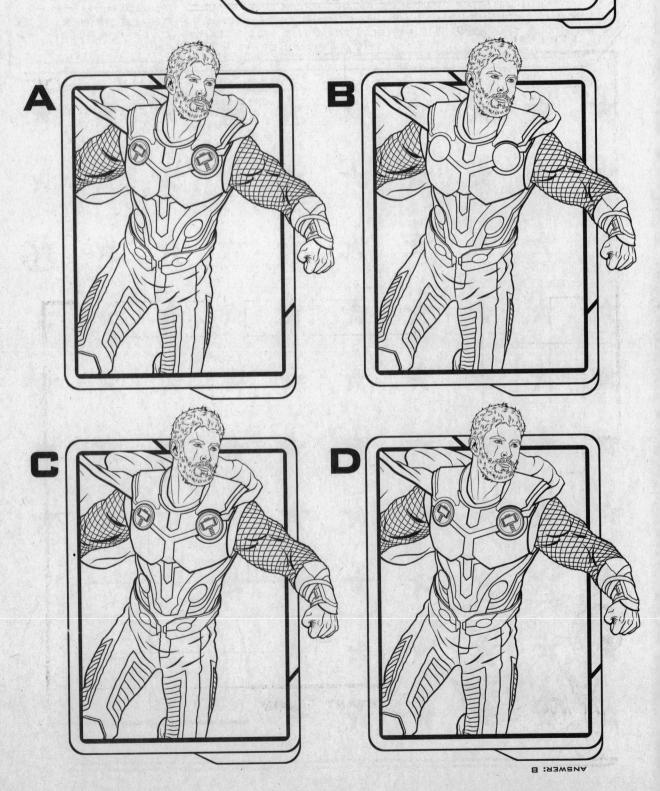

ANSWER: B

MAZE

Guide Black Widow and Captain America through the maze.

FINISH

START

CRACK the CODE

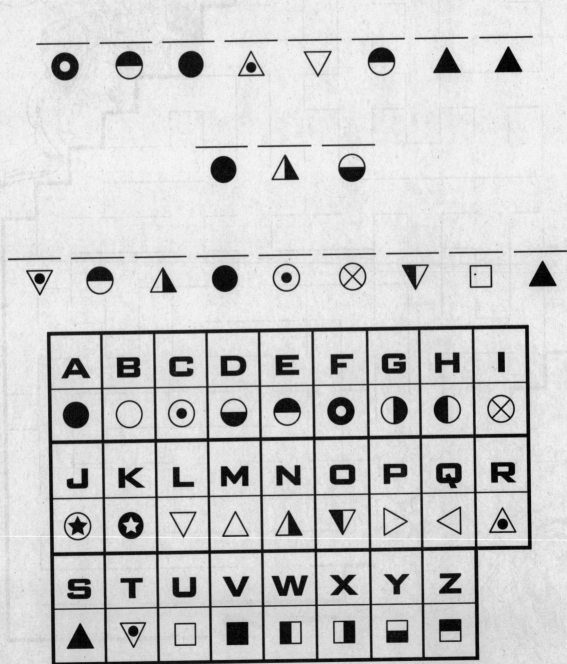

ANSWER: FEARLESS AND TENACIOUS